e **BARON'S** *own projection*

The Baron relates his adventures

12 ADVENTURES OF THE

CELEBRATED

BARON MUNCHAUSEN

selected and illustrated by

BRIAN ROBB

ANDRE DEUTSCH

First published June 1947 by
Peter Lunn (Publishers) Limited
This edition first published 1978 by
André Deutsch Limited
105 Great Russell Street, London wc1

Illustrations copyright © 1947 and 1978 by Brian Robb
All rights reserved

Filmset by Keyspools Ltd, Golborne, Lancs
Printed in Great Britain by
Sackville Press Billericay Ltd

ISBN 0 233 97019 3

First published in the United States of America 1979

Library of Congress number
78-74467

Baron Munchausen's memoirs appeared in several languages, and with many variations, towards the end of the eighteenth century. They have always been famous for the eloquence and imagination with which he describes his unusual experiences, and the Baron must certainly have been one of the most widely travelled beings who ever existed, because his memoirs include, not only descriptions of adventures in most parts of the world we inhabit, but also (in Adventure 11) one of the few complete accounts of a voyage to the Moon.

Of the first six incidents described in this book, five took place in the course of the Baron's expedition to Russia, to fight in the service of the Czar against the forces of the Sultan of Turkey; the seventh on a journey to North America; the eighth when bathing in the Mediterranean; the ninth when travelling in Egypt in the service of the Sultan; the tenth somewhere near the East Indies; and the twelfth off the coast of England, near Spithead. The strange thing is that wherever the Baron travelled, and whatever the object of his journey, he was always pursued by the most remarkable happenings of all kinds.

In his lifetime the Baron was much troubled by the incredulity with which people received his accounts of these occurrences, and unfortunately some readers *do* still cast doubts on their accuracy in detail. In order to anticipate any suspicions which may arise in *your* mind I am including (on page 8 of this book) an exact copy of Baron Munchausen's personal and conclusive rebuttal of imputations of exaggeration or inexactitude.

Brian Robb

TO THE PUBLIC

Having heard, for the first time, that my adventures have been doubted, and looked upon as jokes, I feel bound to come forward and vindicate my character *for veracity*, by paying three shillings at the Mansion House of this great city for the affidavit hereto appended.

This I have been forced into in regard of my own honour, although I have retired for many years from public and private life; and I hope that this, my last edition, will place me in a proper light with my readers.

LONDON

AT THE CITY OF LONDON
ENGLAND

We, the undersigned, as true believers in the profit, do most solemnly hereby affirm, that each and every adventure of **our** friend Baron Munchausen, in whatever country it lies, is a positive and simple fact. **And,** as we have been believed, whose adventures are tenfold more wonderful, **so** do we hope all true believers **will** give Baron

Munchausen

their full faith and credence.

Sworn at the Mansion House
9th November last, in the
absence of the Lord Mayor

Gulliver ✗
Sinbad ✗
Aladdin ✗
John (the Porter)

CONTENTS

Adventure 1

In which the Baron proves himself a good shot

PAGE 13

Adventure 2

The Baron loses his horse and finds a wolf

PAGE 19

Adventure 3

He shoots a stag with cherry stones;
the wonderful effects of it

PAGE 25

Adventure 4

The Baron is presented with a famous horse, with
which he performs extraordinary feats

PAGE 31

Adventure 5

Further extraordinary feats on the part of the
Baron's horse

PAGE 37

Adventure 6

The Baron extricates himself from a carriage
which he meets in a narrow road, in a manner
never before attempted, nor practised since

PAGE 45

Adventure 7

The Baron relates his adventures on a voyage to
North America

PAGE 53

Adventure 8

Bathing in the Mediterranean he meets an
unexpected companion

PAGE 61

Adventure 9

The Baron goes on an embassy to Cairo, and
returns upon the Nile, where he is thrown into an
unexpected situation, and detained six weeks

PAGE 69

Adventure 10

A voyage Eastward. The Baron introduces a friend
who never deceived him, and wins a hundred guineas

PAGE 79

Adventure 11

A visit, albeit accidental, to the Moon.
A description of the inhabitants and their customs
PAGE 87

Adventure 12

The Baron returns to Europe and raises the hull
of the Royal George
PAGE 99

ADVENTURE I

The Baron is riding through Lithuania on his way to St. Petersburg. It is bitterly cold and he is looking for a village in which to pass the night

WENT on: night and darkness overtook me. No village was to be seen. The country was covered with snow and I was unacquainted with the road.

Tired, I alighted, and fastened my horse to something like a pointed stump of a tree, which appeared above the snow; for the sake of safety

I placed my pistols under my arm, and lay down on the snow, where I slept so soundly that I did not open my eyes till full daylight. It is not easy to conceive my astonishment at finding myself in the midst of a village, lying in a churchyard; nor was my horse to be seen, but I heard him soon after neigh somewhere

above me. On looking upwards I beheld him hanging by his bridle to the weathercock of the steeple. Matters were now very plain to me: the village had been covered with snow over-night; a sudden change of weather had taken place; I had sunk down to the churchyard

whilst asleep, gently, and in the same proportion as the snow had melted away; and what in the dark I had taken to be a stump of a little tree, to which I had tied my horse, proved to have been the weathercock of the steeple!

Without long consideration I took one of my pistols, shot the bridle in two, brought down the horse, and proceeded on my journey.

He carried me well – advancing into the interior parts of Russia. I found travelling on horseback rather inconvenient in winter, and I therefore submitted to the custom of the country, took a single horse sledge, and drove briskly towards St. Petersburg.

ADVENTURE 2

*The Baron proceeds on his journey
to St. Petersburg*

IN the midst of a dreary forest I spied a terrible wolf making after me, with all the speed of ravenous winter hunger. He soon overtook me. There was no possibility of escape. Mechanically I laid myself down flat in the sledge, and let my horse run for our safety. What I wished, but hardly hoped or expected, happened immediately after. The wolf did not mind me in the least, but took a leap over me, and falling furiously on the horse, began instantly to tear and devour the hind-part of the

poor animal, which ran the faster for his pain and terror. Thus unnoticed and safe myself, I lifted my head slyly up, and with horror I beheld that the wolf had ate his way into the horse's body; it was not long before he had fairly forced himself into it, when I took my advantage and fell upon him with the butt-end of my whip. This unexpected attack frightened him so much, that he leaped forward with all his might: the horse's carcase dropped on the ground but in his place the wolf was in the

harness, and I on my part whipping him continually: we both arrived in full career safe to St. Petersburg, contrary to our respective expectations, and very much to the astonishment of the spectators.

ADVENTURE 3

The Baron recalls a hunting exploit

AVING one day spent all my shot, I found myself unexpectedly in the presence of a stately stag, looking at me as unconcernedly as if he had known of my empty pouches. I charged immediately with powder, and upon it a good handful of cherry-stones,

for I had sucked the fruit as far as the hurry
would permit. Thus I let fly at him, and hit him
just on the middle of the forehead, between his
antlers; it stunned him – he staggered – yet he
made off. A year or two after, being with a
party in the same forest, I beheld a noble stag
with a fine full-grown cherry-tree about ten

feet high between his antlers. I immediately recollected my former adventure, looked upon him as my property, and brought him to the ground by one shot, which at once gave the haunch and cherry-sauce; for the tree was covered with the richest fruit, the like of which I had never tasted before.

ADVENTURE 4

*While in Russia the Baron visits the house
of a Lithuanian nobleman,
and acquires a remarkable horse*

MY superb Lithuanian horse became mine by an accident, which gave me an opportunity of showing my horsemanship to a great advantage. I was at Count Przobossky's noble country seat in Lithuania, and remained with the ladies at tea in the drawing-room, while the gentlemen were down in the yard, to see a young horse of blood which had just arrived from the stud. We suddenly heard a noise of distress; I hastened downstairs and found the horse so unruly, that nobody durst approach or mount him. The most resolute horsemen stood dismayed and aghast; despondency was expressed in every countenance, when in one leap, I was on his back, took him by surprise, and worked him quite into gentleness

and obedience, with the best display of horse-manship I was master of. Fully to show this to the ladies, and save them unnecessary trouble, I forced him to leap in at one of the open windows of the tea-room, walked round several times, pace, trot, and gallop, and at last made him mount the tea-table, there to repeat his lessons in a pretty style of miniature

which was exceedingly pleasing to the ladies,
for he performed them amazingly well, and
did not break either cup or saucer. It placed me
so high in their opinion, and so well in that of
the noble lord, that, with his usual politeness,
he begged I would accept of the young horse,
and ride him full career to conquest and
honour in the campaign
against the Turks.

ADVENTURE 5

The Baron is employed by the Emperor of Russia in his war against the Turks, and given command of a body of hussars. After a successful engagement in which the enemy are routed, he pursues them into, and through, a walled town

HE swiftness of my Lithuanian enabled me to be foremost in the pursuit; and seeing the enemy fairly flying through the opposite gate, I thought it would be prudent to stop in the market-place, to order the men to rendezvous; but judge of my astonishment when in this market-place I saw not one of my

hussars about me! Are they scouring the streets? They could not be far off, and must, at all events, soon join me. In that expectation I walked my panting Lithuanian to a spring in this market-place, and let him drink. He drank uncommonly, with an eagerness not to be satisfied, but natural enough; for when I

looked round for my men, what should I see, gentlemen! the hind part of the poor creature – croup and legs were missing, as if he had been cut in two, and the water ran out as it came in, without refreshing or doing him any good! How it could have happened was quite a

mystery to me, till I returned with him to the town gate. There I saw, that when I rushed in pell-mell with the flying enemy, they had dropped the portcullis (a heavy falling door, with sharp spikes at the bottom, let down suddenly to prevent the entrance of an enemy

into a fortified town) unperceived by me, which had totally cut off his hind part, that still lay quivering on the outside of the gate. It would have been an irreparable loss, had not our farrier contrived to bring both parts together while hot. He sewed them up with sprigs and young shoots of laurel that were at hand;

the wound healed, and, what could not have happened but to so glorious a horse, the sprigs took root in his body, grew up, and formed a bower over me; so that afterwards I could go upon many other expeditions in the shade of my own and my horse's laurels.

ADVENTURE 6

At the conclusion of the campaign against the Turks, the Baron leaves Russia to return home

AT my return, I felt on the road greater inconveniences than those I had experienced on my setting out.

I travelled post, and finding myself in a narrow lane, bid the boy give a signal with his horn, that other travellers might not meet us in the narrow passage. He blew with all his might; but his endeavours were in vain, he could not make the horn sound, which was unaccountable, and rather unfortunate, for soon after we found ourselves in the presence of another coach coming the other way: there was no proceeding; however I got out of my carriage, and

being pretty strong, placed
it, wheels and all, upon my
head: I then jumped over a hedge
about nine feet high (which considering
the weight of the coach, was rather
difficult) into a field, and came out again
by another jump into the road beyond

the other carriage: I then went back for the horses, and placing one upon my head, and the other under my left arm, by the same means brought them to my coach, put to, and proceeded to an inn at the end of our stage. I should have told you that the horse under my arm was very spirited, and not above four years old; in making my second spring over the hedge, he expressed great dislike to that violent kind of motion by kicking and snorting; however, I confined his hind legs by putting them into my coat-pocket. After we arrived at the inn my coachmen and I refreshed ourselves: the boy hung his horn on a peg near the kitchen fire; I sat on the other side.

Suddenly we heard a *tereng! tereng! teng! teng!* We looked round, and now found the reason why the boy had not been able to sound his horn; his tunes were frozen up in the horn,

and came out now by thawing, plain enough, and much to his credit; so that the honest fellow entertained us for some time with a variety of tunes, without putting his mouth to the horn – The King of Prussia's March – Over the Hill and Over the Dale – with many other favourite tunes.

ADVENTURE 7

The Baron relates his experiences
on a voyage to North America

I EMBARKED at Portsmouth in a first-rate English man-of-war, of one hundred guns, and fourteen hundred men, for North America. Nothing worth relating happened till we arrived within three hundred leagues of the river St. Laurence, when the ship struck with amazing force against (as we supposed) a rock; however, upon heaving the lead we could find no bottom, even with three hundred fathom. What made this circumstance the more wonderful, and indeed beyond all comprehension, was, that the violence of the shock was such that we lost our rudder, broke our bow-sprit in the middle, and split all our masts from top to bottom, two of which went by the board; a poor fellow, who was aloft furling the mainsheet, was flung at least three leagues from the ship; but he fortunately saved his life by laying hold of the tail of a large sea-gull, who brought him back, and lodged him on the very spot from whence he was thrown. Another proof of the violence of the shock was the force with which the people between decks were driven against the floors above them; my head particularly was pressed into my stomach, where it continued some months before it recovered its natural situation. Whilst we were

all in a state of astonishment at the general and
unaccountable confusion in which we were

involved, the whole was suddenly explained by
the appearance of a large whale, who had been

basking, asleep, within sixteen feet of the surface of the water. This animal was so much displeased with the disturbance which our ship had given him, for in our passage we had with

our rudder scratched his nose, that he beat in all the gallery and part of the quarter-deck with his tail, and almost at the same instant took the main-sheet anchor, which was suspended, as it usually is, from the head, between his teeth, and ran away with the ship, at least sixty leagues, at the rate of twelve leagues an hour, when fortunately the cable broke, and we lost both the whale and the anchor. How-

ever, upon our return to Europe, some months after, we found the same whale, within a few leagues of the same spot, floating dead upon the water; it measured above half a mile in length. As we could take but a small quantity of such a monstrous animal on board, we got our boats out, and with much difficulty cut off his head, where, to our great joy, we found the anchor, and above forty fathom of the cable, concealed on the left side of his mouth, just under his tongue.

ADVENTURE 8

*The Baron recalls an unexpected adventure
he experienced when bathing in the sea*

I WAS once in great danger of being lost in a most singular manner in the Mediterranean: I was bathing in that pleasant sea near Marseilles one summer's afternoon, when I discovered a very large fish, with his jaws quite extended, approaching me with the greatest velocity; there was no time to be lost, nor could I possibly avoid him. I immediately reduced myself to as small a size as possible, by closing my feet and placing my hands also near

my sides, in which position I passed directly between his jaws, and into his stomach, where I remained some time in total darkness, and comfortably warm, as you may imagine; at last it occurred to me, that by giving him pain he would be glad to get rid of me: as I had plenty of room, I played my pranks, such as tumbling, hop, step, and jump, etc., but nothing seemed to disturb him so much as the quick motion of my feet in attempting to dance a

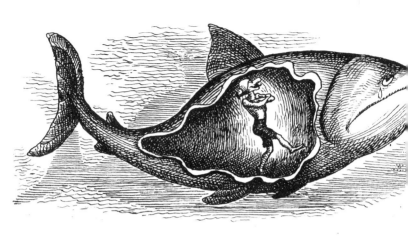

horn-pipe; soon after I began he put me out by sudden fits and starts: I persevered; at last he roared horridly, and stood up almost perpendicularly in the water, with his head and shoulders exposed, by which he was discovered by the people on board an Italian trader, then sailing by, who harpooned him in a few minutes. As soon as he was brought on board I heard the crew consulting how they should cut him up, so as to preserve the greatest quantity of oil. As I understood Italian I was in most dreadful apprehensions lest their

weapons employed in this
business should destroy
me also; therefore I
stood as near the
centre as possible,
for there was room

enough for a dozen men in this creature's stomach, and I naturally imagined they would begin with the extremities: however, my fears were soon dispersed, for they began by opening the bottom of the belly. As soon as I perceived a glimmering of light I called out lustily to be released from a situation in which I was now almost suffocated. It is impossible for me to do justice to the degree and kind of astonishment which sat upon every countenance at hearing a human voice issue from a fish, but more so at seeing a naked man walk upright out of his body; in short, gentlemen, I told them the whole story, as I have done you, whilst amazement struck them dumb.

*　　*　　*

After taking some refreshment, and jumping into the sea to cleanse myself, I swam to my clothes, which lay where I had left them on the

shore, then dressed. As near as I can calculate, I was near four hours and a half confined in the stomach of this animal.

ADVENTURE 9

*The Baron describes a difficulty that arose
when he was conducting an important mission
on behalf of the Sultan of Turkey,
or Grand Seignior*

THE Grand Seignior, to whom I was once introduced by the Imperial

Russian and French ambassadors, employed me to negotiate a matter of great importance at Grand Cairo, and which was of such a nature that it must ever remain a secret.

I went there in great state by land; where having completed the business, I dismissed

almost all my attendants, and returned like a private gentleman: the weather was delightful, and that famous river the Nile was beautiful

beyond all description; in short, I was tempted to hire a barge to descend by water to Alexandria. On the third day of my voyage the river began to rise most amazingly (you have all heard, I presume, of the annual overflowing of the Nile), and on the next day it spread the

whole country for many leagues on each side! On the fifth, at sunrise, my barge became entangled with what I at first took for shrubs, but as the light became stronger I found myself surrounded by almonds, which were perfectly ripe, and in the highest perfection. Upon

plumbing with a line my people found we were at least sixty feet from the ground, and unable to advance or retreat. At about eight or nine o'clock, as near as I could judge by the altitude of the sun, the wind rose suddenly, and canted our barge on one side: here she filled, and I

saw no more of her for some time. Fortunately we all saved ourselves (six men and two boys) by clinging to the tree, the boughs of which were equal to our weight, though not to that of the barge: in this situation we continued six weeks and three days, living upon the almonds; I need not inform you we had plenty of water. On the forty-second day of our distress the water fell as rapidly as it had risen, and on the forty-sixth we were able to venture down upon terra firma. Our barge was the first pleasing object we saw, about two hundred yards from the spot where she sunk. After drying everything that was useful by the heat of the sun, and loading ourselves with necessaries from the stores on board, we set out to recover our lost ground, and found, by the nearest calculation, we had been carried over garden-walls, and a

variety of enclosures, above one hundred and fifty miles. In four days, after a very tiresome journey on foot, with thin shoes, we reached the river, which was now confined to its banks, related our adventures to a boy, who kindly accommodated all our wants, and sent us forward in a barge of his own. In six days more we arrived at Alexandria, where we took shipping for Constantinople. I was received kindly by the Grand Seignior, and had the honour of seeing the seraglio, to which his highness introduced me himself.

ADVENTURE 10

The Baron introduces a friend
who never deceived him

IN a voyage which I made to the East Indies with Captain Hamilton, I took a favourite pointer with me; he was, to use a common phrase, worth his weight in gold, for he never deceived me. One day, when we were, by the best observations we could make, at least three hundred leagues from land, my dog pointed; I observed him for near an hour with astonishment, and mentioned the circumstance to the captain and every officer on board,

asserting that we must be near land, for my dog smelt game. This occasioned a general laugh; but that did not alter in the least the good opinion I had of my dog. After much conversation pro and con, I boldly told the captain I placed more confidence in Tray's nose than I did in the eyes of every seaman on board, and therefore proposed laying the sum I had agreed to pay for my passage (viz., one hundred guineas) that we should find game within half an hour. The captain (a good, hearty fellow) laughed again, desired Mr. Crowford the surgeon, who was prepared, to feel my pulse; he did so, and reported me in perfect health. The following dialogue between them took place; I overheard it, though spoken low, and at some distance.

CAPTAIN. "His brain is turned; I cannot with honour accept his wager."

SURGEON. "I am of a different opinion; he is quite sane, and depends more upon the scent of his dog than he will upon the judgement of all the officers on board; he will certainly lose, and he richly merits it."

CAPTAIN. "Such a wager cannot be fair on my side; however, I'll take him up, if I return his money afterwards."

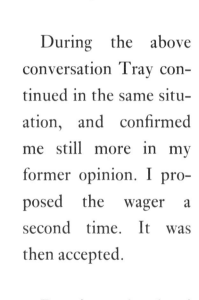

During the above conversation Tray continued in the same situation, and confirmed me still more in my former opinion. I proposed the wager a second time. It was then accepted.

Done! and done! were scarcely said on

both sides, when some sailors who were fishing in the long-boat, which was made fast to the stern of the ship harpooned an exceedingly large shark, which they brought on board and began to cut up for the purpose of barrelling the oil, when, behold, they found no less than *six brace*

of live partridges in this animal's stomach!
They had been so long in that situation, that
one of the hens was sitting upon four eggs, and
a fifth was hatching when the shark was
opened!!! This young bird we brought up by
placing it with a litter of kittens that came into

the world a few minutes before! The old cat was as fond of it as of any of her four-legged progeny, and made herself very unhappy when it flew out of her reach, till it returned again.

ADVENTURE 11

*The Baron tells the story of his successful
(but accidental) visit to the Moon*

N the eighteenth day after we had passed the Island of Otaheite, mentioned by Captain Cook as the place from whence they brought Omai, a hurricane blew our ship at least one thousand leagues above the surface of the water, and kept it at that height till a fresh gale arising filled the sails in every part, and onwards we travelled at a

prodigious rate; thus we proceeded above the clouds for six weeks. At last we discovered a great land in the sky, like a shining island, round and bright, where, coming into a convenient harbour, we went on shore, and soon found it was inhabited. Below us we saw another earth containing cities, trees, mountains, rivers, seas, etc., which we conjectured was this world which we had left. Here we saw huge figures riding upon vultures of a prodigious size, and each of them having three heads. To form some idea of the magnitude of these birds, I must inform you that each of

their wings is as wide and six
times the length of the main sheet
of our vessel, which was about six hundred tons burthen. Thus, instead of riding
upon horses, as we do in this world, the inhabitants of the moon (for we now found we

were in Madam Luna) fly about on these birds. The king, we found, was engaged in a war with the sun, and he offered me a commission, but I declined the honour he intended. Everything in *this* world is of extraordinary magnitude! a common flea being much larger than one of our sheep: in making war their principal weapons are radishes, which are used as darts: those who are wounded by them die immediately. Their shields are made of mushrooms, and their darts (when radishes are out of season) of the tops of asparagus. Some of the natives of the dog-star are to be seen here; commerce tempts them to ramble; their faces are like large mastiffs', with their eyes near the lower end or tip of their noses: they have no eyelids but cover their eyes with the ends of their tongues when they go to sleep; they are generally twenty feet high. As to the natives of the moon, none of them are less in stature than thirty-six feet. They lose no time at their meals, as they open their left side, and place the whole quantity at once in their stomach, then shut it again till the same day in the next month; for they never indulge themselves with food more than twelve times a year, or once a month. All but gluttons and epicures must prefer this method to ours.

They have but one finger upon each hand, with which they perform everything in as perfect a manner as we do who have four besides the thumb. Their heads are placed under their right arm, and when they are going to travel, or about any violent exercise, they generally leave them at home, for they can consult them at any distance.

Their eyes can take in and out of their places when they please, and can see as well

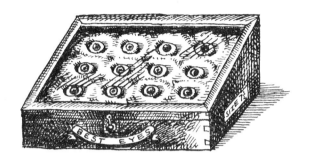

with them in their hand as in their head! and if by any accident they lose or damage one, they can borrow or purchase another, and see as clearly with it as their own. Dealers in eyes are on that account very numerous in most parts of the moon, and in this article alone all the inhabitants are whimsical: sometimes green and sometimes yellow eyes are the fashion. I

know these things appear strange; but if the shadow of a doubt can remain on any person's mind, I say, let him take voyage there himself, and then he will know I am a traveller of veracity.

ADVENTURE 12

*The Baron salvages
the famous English man-of-war,
the Royal George
which sank off Spithead in 1782*

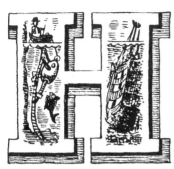EARING so many persons talk about raising the *Royal George*, I began to take pity on that fine old ruin of English plank, and determined to have her up. I was sensible of the failure of the various means hitherto employed for the purpose, and therefore inclined to try a method different from any before attempted. I got an immense balloon, made of the toughest sail-cloth, and having descended in my diving-bell, and properly secured the hull with enormous cables, I ascended to the surface, and fastened my cables to the balloon. Prodigious multitudes were assembled to behold the elevation of the

Royal George, and as soon as I began to fill my balloon with inflammable air the vessel evidently began to move: but when my balloon was completely filled, she carried up the *Royal George* with the greatest rapidity. The vessel appearing on the surface occasioned a universal shout of triumph from the millions assembled on the occasion. Still the balloon con-

tinued ascending, trailing the hull after like a lantern at the tail of a kite, and in a few minutes appeared floating among the clouds.

It was then the opinion of many philosophers that it would be more difficult to get her down that it had been to draw her up, but I convinced them to the contrary by taking my aim so exactly with a twelve-pounder, that I brought her down in an instant.

I considered, that if I should break the balloon with a cannon-ball while she remained with the vessel over the land, the fall would inevitably occasion the destruction of the hull, which in its fall might crush some of the multitude; therefore I thought it safer to take my aim when the balloon was over the sea, and pointing my twelve-pounder, drove the ball right through the balloon, on which the inflammable air rushed out with great force, and the *Royal George* descended like a falling star into the very spot from whence she had been taken. There she still remains and I have convinced all Europe of the possibility of taking her up.

A PICTURE

Drawn to the direction of the

facilitate the st

Brian Robb delineavit

drawn to scale